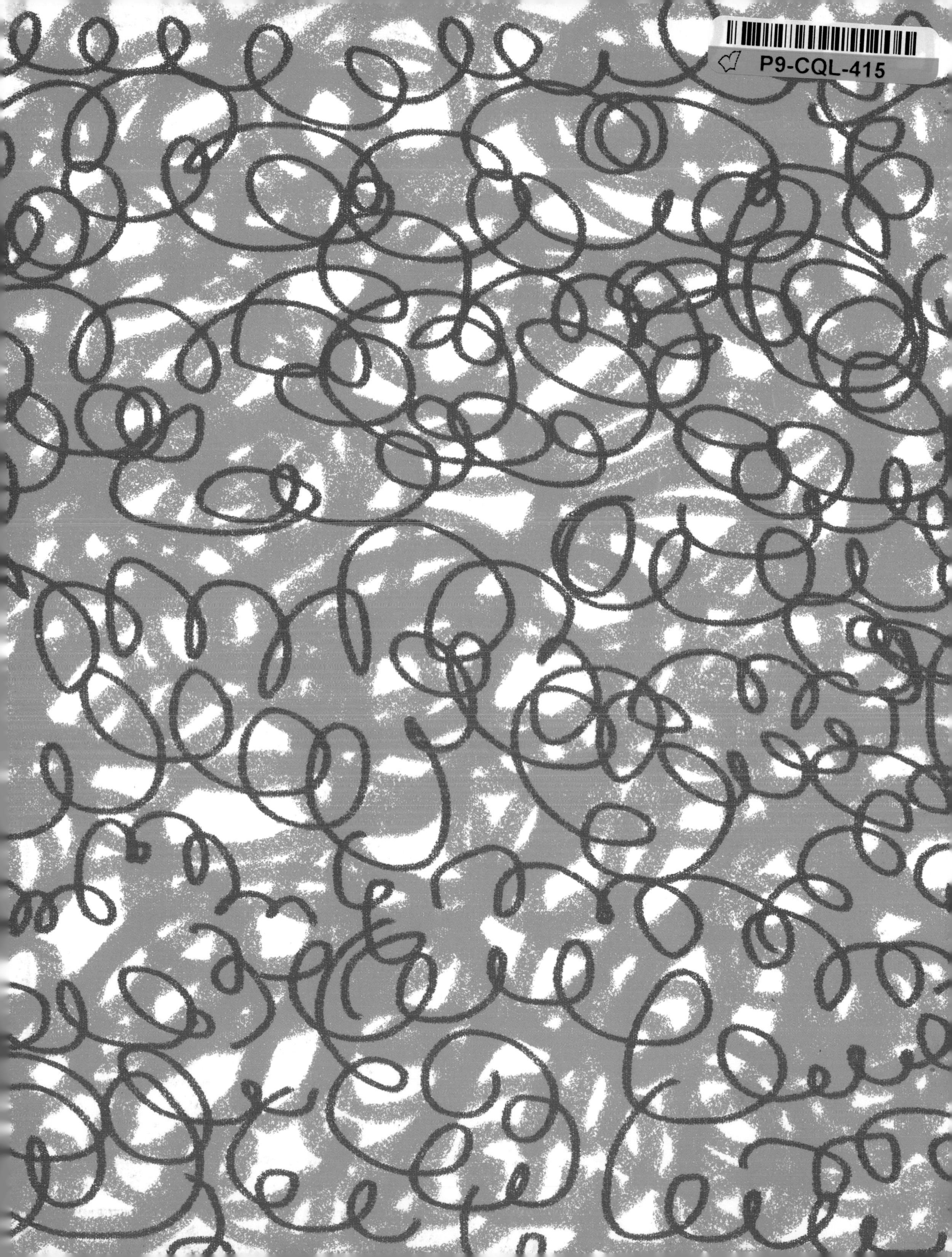
P9-CQL-415

CIP Data is available.
Published in the
United States 2006 by
Blue Apple Books
P.O. Box 1380,
Maplewood, N.J. 07040
www.blueapplebooks.com
Distributed in the U.S.
by Chronicle Books
First Edition
Printed in
China

ISBN 13: 978-1-59354-161-3
ISBN 10: 1-59354-161-9

1 3 5 7 9 10 8 6 4 2

There Was a Little Girl, She Had a Little Curl

Harriet Ziefert

Pictures by Elliot Kreloff

For Sylvie Anne
–H.Z.

For Sophia
–E.K.

There was a little girl
and she had a little curl,
right in the middle of her forehead.

When she was good,
she was very, very good.
And when she was bad,
she was . . .

Isabel was her name.

Isabel lived with her mother, her father,
her dog, Oliver, and her cat, Lulu.

One Saturday morning,
Isabel woke up and said,

She did not disturb her parents.
She did not turn on the television.

Isabel got dressed
and went to the kitchen.

She moved the cat.

She prepared a bowl
of cereal for herself
and ate it all up.
And she did not
use her sleeve as
a napkin—
not even once.

Then she let
the dog out.

After breakfast,
Isabel decided to play dress-up.

When she heard her mother say,

**Isabel!
It's time to go
shopping for
sneakers.**

she went downstairs right away.

Isabel was good. Very good.

She didn't complain
when her mother said that
the white sneakers would
get too dirty,

or that the sneakers
with blinking lights
didn't fit well,

or that the pink ones
with jewels
were too fancy.

She agreed that the plain blue ones
were the best and happily wore them home.

Nails

Isabel was proud of her new shoes.
She wanted to show them to Lulu and Oliver,
but she didn't know where they were.
So she went to her mom's room to see
if they were hiding under the dressing table.

Isabel sat in her mom's chair.

She put on lipstick . . .

and rouge . . .

and powder . . .

and even eye shadow.

She tried to polish her nails, but it was hard to keep from painting her fingers, so she stopped.

Then Isabel tried to fix her hair.
She struggled with the comb and the brush . . . and it hurt!
She wished she didn't have so much hair.

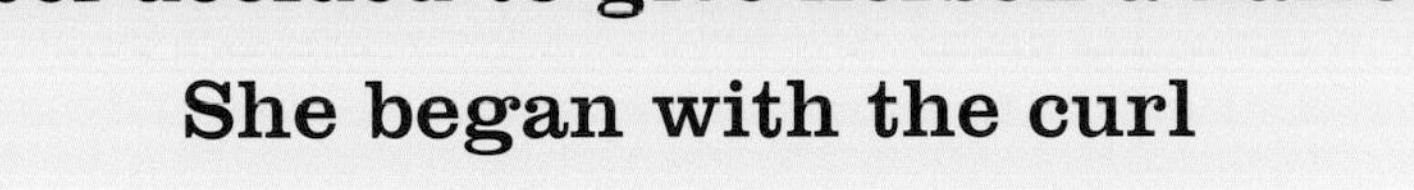

Isabel decided to give herself a haircut.
She began with the curl
in the middle of her forehead.

Then she cut
another curl,

and another,

and another,

and still another curl.

She heard her mother calling.

Isabel quickly wiped her face
with her sleeve and went downstairs.

Isabel, what happened to your hair?
I didn't mean to cut it! It was an accident.

Then Isabel began to cry:

I look HORRID!

I don't want Daddy to see me.

I can't make your hair look any better, but if you stop crying, we can go to the beauty shop and see if someone there can repair the damage.

HAIR

Isabel got a haircut.
SNIP
SNIP

At dinner that night, Isabel thought her daddy would notice her haircut and be angry. But he wasn't. He just asked,

Isabel said,
"I played dress-up with Oliver.
I ate everything on my plate, even the beets.
I got new blue sneakers.
AND I got a haircut!"

Isabel's mommy
didn't say a word.

I am a little girl
and I had a little curl,
right in the middle
of my forehead.
When I am good,
I am very, very good.
And when I am bad,
I am horrid!

Good-night, Isabel.